I WANT TO KNOW

Was Count Dracula Real?

Heather Moore Niver

Enslow Publishing
101 W. 23rd Street
Suite 240
New York, NY 10011
USA
enslow.com

Published in 2018 by Enslow Publishing, LLC.
101 W. 23rd Street, Suite 240, New York, NY 10011

Library of Congress Cataloging-in-Publication Data

Names: Niver, Heather Moore, author.
Title: Was Count Dracula real? / Heather Moore Niver.
Description: New York, NY : Enslow Publishing, 2018. | Series: I want to know | Includes bibliographical references and index. | Audience: Grades 3-5
Identifiers: LCCN 2017012000| ISBN 9780766091962 (library bound) | ISBN 9780766093706 (pbk.) | ISBN 9780766093713 (6 pack)
Subjects: LCSH: Vlad III, Prince of Wallachia, 1430 or 1431-1476 or 1477—Juvenile literature. | Wallachia—Kings and rulers—Biography—Juvenile literature. | Wallachia—History—Juvenile literature. | Dracula, Count (Fictitious character)—Juvenile literature.
Classification: LCC DR240.5.V553 N58 2017 | DDC 949.8/014092 [B] —dc23
LC record available at https://lccn.loc.gov/2017012000

Printed in China

To Our Readers: We have done our best to make sure all websites in this book were active and appropriate when we went to press. However, the author and the publisher have no control over and assume no liability for the material available on those websites or on any websites they may link to. Any comments or suggestions can be sent by email to customerservice@enslow.com.

Photo Credits: Cover diversepixel/Shutterstock.com; pp. 3, 26 Emi Cristea/Shutterstock.com; p. 5 Universal History Archive/Universal Images Group/Getty Images; pp. 6, 27 (top and bottom) Bettmann/Getty Images; p. 8 Universal Pictures/Moviepix/Getty Images; p. 9 Kiselev Andrey Valerevich/Shutterstock.com; p. 11 Heritage Images/Hulton Fine Art Collection/Getty Images; p. 13 Herbert Barraud/Hulton Archive/Getty Images; p. 14 Pierre Verdy/AFP/Getty Images; p. 15 © Look and Learn/Bridgeman Images; p. 17 Paul Fearn/Alamy Stock Photo; p. 19 Jareso/Shutterstock.com; p. 20 breakermaximus/Shutterstock.com; p. 23 Science History Images/Alamy Stock Photo.

Contents

Chapter 1

Meet the Count

Count Dracula prowls in the shadows. Most people think of a man with pale skin and pointy teeth and ears. He wears a formal black cape. His home is a creepy castle located deep in the mountains of Transylvania. Mysterious Count Dracula only comes out at night. Count Dracula is one of the most famous characters in the world. Could such a frightening figure be a real person?

Stoker's Scary Story

People have been telling stories about vampires for thousands of years. But it wasn't until the 1800s

Imagine That!

Count Dracula is one of the "undead." This means he is dead, but still moving and walking around.

Actor Bela Lugosi played the undead count in the 1931 movie *Dracula*, frightening audiences everywhere.

Vampire Poetry

The first vampire poem to be published was called "The Vampyre." It was written by a doctor named John Polidori in 1819. Polidori wrote it when he was with writers Lord Byron, Percy Shelley, and Shelley's soon-to-be wife Mary. Byron proposed a friendly competition to the group. Everyone should write a ghost story. Lord Byron started to write a story about vampires but never finished it. Mary Shelley ended up starting the famous novel *Frankenstein*.

and 1900s that people really started to use the word "vampire." Vampires could be the most popular monsters in the world now.

Irish author Bram Stoker (1847–1912) wrote his famous scary story in 1897. He titled it *Dracula*. It became the most popular book

Bram Stoker wrote one of the most famous vampire stories ever told: *Dracula*.

about vampires. And it changed the way people think of vampires. Many books, television shows, and movies use Count Dracula as their model to this day.

Stoker tells the story in a unique way. Different characters write letters, diary entries, and telegrams (messages sent by wire). Jonathan Harker is hired to work for Count Dracula. Harker soon realizes that the count is mysterious. Dracula never has a shadow or a reflection in a mirror. The count is incredibly strong. He can shape-shift, or change shape, into a bat or wolf to escape when he needs to. He could also turn into clouds or mist to get into locked rooms. He slips through keyholes or under doors. The count can even hypnotize people.

Eventually Dracula turns Harker's friend Lucy Westenra into a vampire. He even falls in love with Harker's own wife, Mina. Dr. John Seward helps Harker kill the count.

Dracula is a **gothic novel**. In this horror mystery story, Count Dracula needs fresh blood to live. He

Dracula (Bela Lugosi) attempts to hypnotize a man (Lou Costello) in the 1948 comedy *Abbott and Costello Meet Frankenstein.*

goes out at night and looks for living people to bite. Did Stoker get his ideas from real life? Or did he make everything up?

I Dream of Dracula

People have many interesting ideas about how the story started. One idea is that Stoker woke up in the middle

The fanged female in *Carmilla* may have inspired Stoker, who may have dreamt about a vampire rising from a tomb when he began his tale.

of the night from a terrible nightmare. He dreamt that a vampire rose from its **tomb**.

Stoker may have read a novel by Joseph Sheridan Le Fanu called *Carmilla,* about a female vampire. But the bloodthirsty Carmilla is not Stoker's only **inspiration**. Some real-life people helped Stoker create his famous story.

Chapter 2

Violent Vlad III

Most people think that Dracula was the ruler Vlad III Dracula (1431–1476). He was also called Vlad Tepes or Vlad III, prince of Wallachia. (Wallachia is now known as the country of Romania.)

Vlad III was not a vampire. In fact, he was known as a good leader. Even today, he is remembered for keeping his people safe. But he could be cruel and violent. Vlad III may have even killed anywhere between forty thousand to a hundred thousand people!

Imagine That!

At first, Bram Stoker named his main character Count Wampyr. He probably changed it after reading about Vlad Dracula.

Although stories claiming that Vlad III was a vampire were untrue, his violent behavior may have inspired Stoker's story.

What Was at Stake?

Vlad's life has some colorful details that might have inspired Stoker's scary story. Some stories claimed that Vlad ate his victims and drank their blood! He was known for stabbing his victims. Then he would impale their bodies on stakes. Vlad may have used wooden stakes to stab his victims. Vlad's method might have inspired Stoker's idea of killing a vampire with a stake. Lucy is killed with a stake in Stoker's story. (But Count Dracula is not.)

A lot of the stories about Vlad may have been exaggerated. Vlad may have done some of these terrible things, but he may not have been as violent as the stories say he was. The leaders of Germany were his enemies. They might have published information about Vlad to make him sound evil. One pamphlet was called "The Frightening and Truly Extraordinary Story of a Wicked Blood-Drinking **Tyrant** Called Prince Dracula." They may be the reason he got the reputation for drinking blood. Vlad III may have forced people to eat one another, but there is no proof that he drank blood.

He's Got the Look

When we think of Count Dracula now, we usually picture him with **characteristics** such as pointed ears; sharp, pointed teeth; and pale skin. Stoker may have seen wood-cut images of Vlad III and modeled the count after this image.

Stoker also knew an actor named Henry Irving (1838–1905). Irving's appearance may have given Stoker ideas for the look of the count, too. The actor was tall, attractive, and showy. He had long fingers and an intense gaze. In fact, Stoker asked Irving to play the part of Dracula on stage. Irving refused.

Actor Henry Irving's piercing stare and long fingers are just a few things that may have inspired Dracula.

Dracula the Sequel

In 2009, a sequel, or follow-up, to *Dracula* showed up on store shelves. Stoker's great-grandnephew, Dacre Stoker, together with Ian Holt, wrote *Dracula: The Un-Dead*. They created it using notes from the original book. Bram Stoker is a character in this novel. It is set in 1912 in London, England.

Devil or Dragon?

It is unlikely that Dracula was based on Vlad's actions. He was already working on his novel when he read about

Vlad III. Stoker's notes leave a clue. His notes include one of Vlad's nicknames: Dracula.

Vlad III's father was in a group called Order of the Dragon. In the Romanian language, *Dracul* can mean "devil" or "dragon." And *Dracula* means "son of Dracul." Most of the time, the name was linked to the dragon meaning. But some people could not forget that it also meant devil. This may have been especially true when Vlad III acted with such violence.

Vlad's enemies may have started nasty rumors about him, including suggesting he drank human blood.

Chapter 3

The Blood Countess

Not everyone thinks that Count Dracula was modeled after Vlad Tepes. But that does not mean Bram Stoker was not inspired by the living for his undead character.

Blood Baths

Countess Elizabeth Báthory de Ecsed lived from 1560 to 1614 in Hungary. Some call her the Blood Countess. Stoker may have learned about Elizabeth Báthory in his research. An obvious comparison to Count Dracula was that Báthory was a countess. (Unlike Vlad, who was a prince.) Also Báthory was Hungarian, just like Count Dracula. (Vlad, however, lived in Romania.)

Countess Elizabeth Báthory de Ecsed was also known as the Blood Countess because of her violent behavior.

Countess Elizabeth Báthory is often compared to Vlad III. Both were very violent. Báthory may have killed and tortured between 80 and 650 women! Stories say that she killed while her husband was off to war. Báthory would coax poor young women from nearby towns to her castle. She told them they could work for her as servants. Once they were at her castle, she tortured them. The countess may have collected their blood in her bathtub so she could soak in it.

Imagine That!
Elizabeth Báthory may have also been accused of being a witch.

Forever Young

Báthory thought these blood baths would help her stay youthful forever. Where did she come up with this idea? According to legend, Báthory once hit one of her young servants very hard. The servant started to bleed. The girl's blood splashed all over. Before the countess could wipe it off her own skin, she stopped. She noticed something interesting. She thought her

It was said that Báthory lured her victims to her castle, near the village of Čachtice in Slovakia, with the promise of employment.

own skin now looked smooth and young. It looked like her servant's skin. Báthory believed that the blood had healing powers and could make her young again. And this is how she began her bloody activities. Some stories say Báthory bit the girls and drank their blood. Some of her servants helped Báthory murder these young women.

More than three hundred people reportedly **witnessed** or survived her horrible actions. She may have kept a diary of her murders. (But it has never been found.) An official investigation took place. Báthory and her servants were arrested on

Was the Woman a Werewolf?

Some stories refer to Báthory as a werewolf. Tales of this wild woman describe her using her teeth to tear into skin. Stoker may have been inspired by a werewolf description for the count, too. Dracula's short hairy hands and long nails may have come from the book he read about Countess Báthory.

December 30, 1609. The servants were executed in 1611. Elizabeth Báthory was imprisoned in her own castle, where she died.

Later research suggests that Báthory may not have done any of it. Similar to what happened to Vlad III, Báthory's enemies may have made it all up! They just wanted people to think she was a terrible person.

The Countess and the Count

Perhaps Stoker liked the idea of Báthory's blood healing. Some historians think so. Count Dracula seems to look younger each time he drinks blood. At the beginning of the story, the count is a white-haired old man. Later in the book, after drinking blood, he appears much younger and healthier. His hair is darker. His skin looks fresh, too. He can walk out in the daylight again. It's hard to know for sure if the bloody stories are true. We may never know. Did Elizabeth Báthory's story inspire Stoker? That is another mystery.

Chapter 4

More Horror Lore

Count Dracula was not the first vampire. Stories about blood sucking creatures have been told for thousands of years! Bram Stoker probably used bits and pieces of information from many different places. He put them all together to write *Dracula*.

Lilith and Lamatsu

Stoker probably knew about some famous vampire **lore**. Lilith is a demon in Jewish mythology. Some religions say she was the very first woman. Stories say Lilith was created even before Eve from the Bible. Other people call her a vampire. She flirted with men and then drank their blood.

Stories about Lilith describe her as a woman with wings and claws who drank blood.

Another source for Stoker's vampire may have been the **Mesopotamian** goddess Lamatsu, whose story is four thousand years old. She killed young men and drank their blood, too. Sometimes she stole babies at night. Some people blamed her for diseases, the deaths of babies, and nightmares.

Lilith and Lamatsu are both described as part animal and part woman, having wings and claws. Both are blamed for stealing children in the night.

Scary Science

Sometimes people made up vampire stories to explain mysteries. This helped them understand things like **corpses**, or dead bodies. For example, after death, the skin dries up and shrinks back. Teeth and fingernails stick out from the shrunken skin and look longer. So the teeth looked more like fangs, and the fingernails looked more like claws. Centuries ago, people did not know that. When they saw a dead body with long nails and teeth, they blamed it on vampirism.

Groans from the Grave

A dead body fills up with gases over time. In the Middle Ages, a lot of people got a disease called tuberculosis. People with the disease were called "walking corpses." They blamed the first person they knew who came down with it. This person was considered a vampire. When they drove a stake through the heart, the gases made noise. It sounded like a groan from the corpse! The body even moved. This was the gases leaving the body. It looked like the dead body was living again!

The Transylvania Connection

Some experts think that Stoker learned about Transylvania from a professor named Arminius Vamberry. Vamberry told Stoker all about his exciting travels to far-off places such as Transylvania. Stoker liked the mysterious-sounding place, with its mountains and castles. (Vamberry also told Stoker about how real-life, undead blood-drinking monsters called vampires may have lived there.) The novel's famous vampire expert is Professor Abraham Van Helsing. Stoker may have modeled him after Vamberry.

Bran Castle is one of the only castles located in the mountains of Transylvania, so it is associated with Stoker's story.

Live Action Vampires

Many modern books, movies, and television shows feature gorgeous vampires. Some of them sparkle in the sunlight, such as in the Twilight books and movies.

Imagine That!
The Count on the television show *Sesame Street* is lightly based on Count Dracula.

Actor Max Schreck played the part of the vampire Count Orlock in the 1922 movie *Nosferatu*. Schreck played a much scarier monster than Dracula, though.

He was so good that people thought he might be an actual vampire! In real life, he had a strange sense of humor. Sometimes he walked in the woods by himself at night. He also created creepy realistic costumes and makeup. These things all added to the vampire rumors.

Bela Lugosi made Count Dracula famous in 1930. Lugosi was romantic and dramatic. He was from Hungary, so he had an accent.

Max Schreck played one of the creepiest counts in the 1922 film *Nosferatu*.

Bela Lugosi created the classic Dracula look with a formal tuxedo and cape.

He had his dark hair slicked back with a widow's peak, sharp fangs, and an intense glare. He wore a black tuxedo and flowing cape. This came to be known as the classic look for the Count Dracula we know and love.

Like the mysterious creature itself, it seems that the fascination with vampires will live forever.

Words to Know

characteristic A special feature that makes someone or something stand out from the rest.

corpse The dead body of a human.

gothic novel A type of mystery and horror novel that became popular in the eighteenth and nineteenth centuries.

inspiration Something that causes a feeling or action.

lore Traditions or information about a specific subject.

Mesopotamian Relating to the ancient civilization that existed between the Tigris and Euphrates Rivers in the Middle East.

tomb A huge vault used to bury the dead, often underground.

tyrant An extremely cruel ruler.

witness To see an event, such as a crime.

Further Reading

Books

Castellano, Peter. *Vampires*. New York, NY: Gareth Stevens, 2016.

Francis, Pauline (adapter). *Dracula*. London, UK: ReadZone Books, 2013.

Keppeler, Jill. *Elizabeth Bathory: The Blood Countess*. New York, NY: Gareth Stevens, 2017.

Shea, John. *Vlad the Impaler*. New York, NY: Gareth Stevens, 2017.

Websites

Bran Castle

bran-castle.com/index.html

Learn about the castle that inspired Count Dracula's home.

Learnodo Newtonic, Dracula

learnodo-newtonic.com/dracula-facts

Check out ten fun facts about the creepy Count Dracula.

PBS, Dracula: The Metamorphosis of a Fiend

www.pbs.org/frontlineworld/stories/romania/dracula1.html

Dive deeper into the folklore of Dracula.

Index